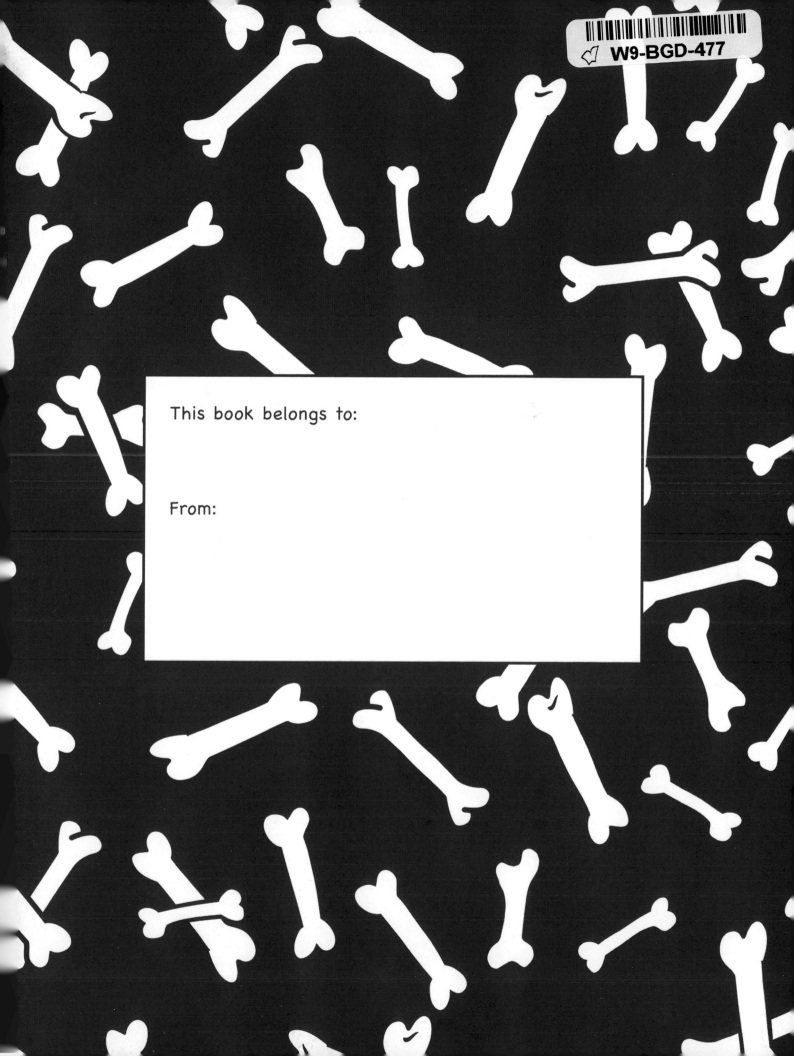

This book belongs to:

From:

Copyright © 2018 Kristi Soli

Published by Evale Publishers

ISBN: 978-0-692-11922-8

Library of Congress Control Number: 2018905753

Any references to historical events, real people, or real places are used fictitiously. Names, characters, and places are products of the author's imagination.

Illustrations by Sharon Wagner.

Book design by Jeff Schalles.

Printed by Bang Printing, Brainerd, MN, in the United States of America.

Category | Children's | Social Situations

First Edition

evalepublishers.com

Mrs. Jones' Tea Party

by
Kristi B. Soli

Illustrated by
Sharon Wagner

Evale Publishers
Edina, Minnesota

For My Beloved Nicholas and Dana

"Mrs. Jones, Mrs. Jones, would you like some cookie bones?" asks the nice Artist Lady, who wears a flowered hat.

That is what she calls me, Mrs. Jones, and I do love cookie bones.

Hello,

I am Mrs. Jones, a black sheep herding dog with curly hair and a curly tail.

I am a little dog that thinks big.

"Yes," I say as I wag my tail.

"Yes please, yes!

I would love some cookie bones."

5

The nice Artist Lady with the flowered hat
bends down and gives me a cookie bone.

I am so happy.

6

I am so happy that I think I will have a tea party and share my cookie bones with my friends.

I'll go ask Tiger, my yellow bird friend, if she would like to help me.

7

"Tiger, oh Tiger...

Will you help me throw a tea party so we can share our cookie bones with our friends?"

"Chirp! Tweet!

Yes, Mrs. Jones. I would love to help you with a tea party.

Chirp! Tweet! What can I help you with?"

"We can make beautiful invitations and decorations.

I will ask if the Artist Lady will help.

This will be wonderful to sit in a beautiful garden, share great food, and visit with wonderful friends."

"Chirp! Tweet! This will be fun to have a tea party."

"Let me go ask the Artist Lady if she wants to help.

Bye, bye, Tiger."

"Tweet! Chirp!"

Off Mrs. Jones goes to see the
Artist Lady.

"Hello, Artist Lady. What a beautiful hat."

"Thank you," said the Artist Lady.

10

"I am going to have a tea party and would like to know if you would help. Tiger is already helping me with the invitations."

"I would love to help. I can get the supplies and prepare and serve the food and tea."

"That would be so helpful. Thank you very much. Now, I am off to ask Nicki the terrier if she will help with the decorations. Thank you again."

Off Mrs. Jones goes to see Nicki the terrier.

Down the walkway, Mrs. Jones travels
to go find Nicki.

I wonder what we should serve and
who we should invite, she thinks
to herself. I'll talk to Tiger.
She always has good ideas.

Whoosh!

Out in front of Mrs. Jones
runs a silly gray squirrel and
off he disappears.

13

Oh! There is Nicki playing ball.

"Hi Nicki, Hi Nicki.

How are you?"

"Woof! Woof! Playing catch. Would you like to play?"

"No thank you. Do you have time to talk?"

"Woof! Woof! Sure. What's up?"

"I am having a tea party and wondering if you would like to help decorate?"

"Woof! Woof! Tea party? Woof! Woof! Will there be cookie bones?"

"Oh, yes! A lot of them."

Wag! Wag!

"Count me in."

"Great, Nicki. I will let you know more later. Now, I am going home to work on invitations with Tiger, the yellow bird."

"Woof! Woof! Have a great day."

Wag! Wag!

"You too."

Off Mrs. Jones goes to see Tiger.

On her walk back she thinks to herself, how shall we decorate? What shall I wear? What should we serve?"

Whoosh!

The silly gray squirrel runs right in front of Mrs. Jones tickling the tip of her nose.

That silly Jax the gray squirrel, Mrs. Jones thinks as she smiles and continues on her way.

"Tiger! Tiger! Are you ready to help with invitations?"

"Chirp! Tweet! Sure. I have ribbon and doilies to make them pretty."

"Let's get busy," Mrs. Jones says as she places the decorations on the table.

"Tweet! Tweet!"

"What do you think about decorations, Tiger?"

"I love the color pink—Tweet!"

"So do I, and I love flowers. Pink and flowers is how it shall be.

Who should we invite, Tiger?"

"I think Midnight, the hamster. He is very quiet and is very shy. I love his company."

"Yes, he is lovely. There is a silly gray squirrel named Jax that loves to hide and when I walk by he loves to run across my path then disappear. I think we should invite him."

"Tweet! Tweet!"

"Okay, so we have

Nicki the terrier;

Midnight the hamster;

Jax the squirrel;

you, Tiger, the bird;

and me, Mrs. Jones, the sheepdog."

"That sounds perfect,
a total of one, two,
three, four, five.

Five it is."

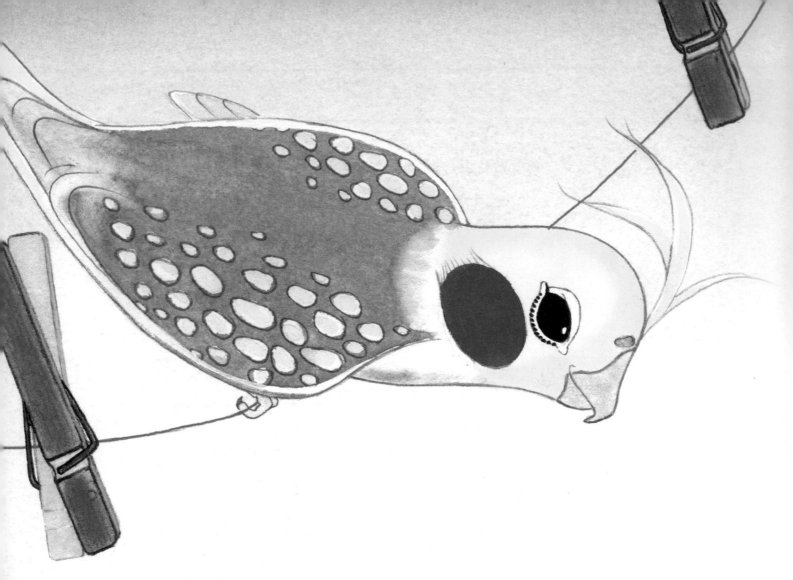

What shall we serve, Tiger?"

"Chirp! I like birdseed. My favorite is sunflower seed."

"Yes, and Nicki loves cookie bones. I think Jax likes nuts and seeds and Midnight likes carrots."

"Chirp! I like carrots and nuts."

"I like carrots too. I think Nicki would too. It sounds like a lovely spread. Nuts, seeds, carrots, and, of course, cookie bones. I am going to tell the Artist Lady what we need for our tea party and drop off these beautiful invitations. Bye, bye. Thank you for your help."

"Chirp. Tweet."

Off Mrs. Jones goes to see the Artist Lady.

"Artist Lady with the beautiful hat, I have the list of things we would like for our tea party," Mrs. Jones says excitedly.

"Mrs. Jones, have a seat and some cookie bones. What do you need?"

"We need seeds, nuts, carrots and a lot of cookie bones. We would like pink and white flowers and decorations. Nicki and Tiger will be helping the day of the tea party."

"I will stop and pick that up for you."

"Thank you. One more thing. May I borrow your hat for the tea party? It is so beautiful. I will let you think about that as I'm off to deliver these invitations. Thank you again."

"My pleasure."

Off Mrs. Jones goes to see Nicki.

As Mrs. Jones is walking down
the trail, she sees Jax hiding.

I am going to pretend I don't
see him and let him have some
fun, she thinks to herself.

Whoosh!

He runs right under
Mrs. Jones chin. So close
that his tail swipes her cheek.

He sure is a squirrel, Mrs. Jones
thinks with a smile.

Mrs. Jones spots Nicki playing with
his friends and keeps walking.

27

"Nicki, Nicki, come here please."

"Woof! Woof! Hello, Mrs. Jones. How are you?"

"Good, good. I won't keep you, but I want to give you this invitation to the tea party. You may open it at home."

"Woof! Woof!"

Wag! Wag!

"Thank you, Mrs. Jones."

"Oh, and don't forget to come early to help decorate."

"I'll be there. Woof!"

He runs off to play.

Mrs. Jones begins to walk back as she sees Jax hiding again getting ready to play his game of hide and surprise.

Watch this, she thinks. I'm going to pretend I don't see him and play a trick on him this time.

Jax comes running out of his hiding spot behind the tree heading straight toward Mrs. Jones. Right before Jax reaches Mrs. Jones, she turns toward him.

Thump, thump, thump.

Jax does three full back somersaults and runs up the tree chattering. Mrs. Jones has stopped him in his tracks.

"Ch, ch, ch, ch, ch!" Jax chatters at Mrs. Jones from the treetop.

Mrs. Jones smiles and says, "Hey Jax, I got you. I'm leaving an invitation here for you. Will you please come to my tea party? I would love to introduce you to my friends."

"Ch, ch, ch, ch, ch!" is all she hears.

The Day of the Tea Party

Ding dong—the doorbell rings.

"Welcome, Nicki. Come on in. We are just getting the tea and treats ready. How are you?"

"Woof! Woof!" Wag! Wag!

"Come in and meet my dear friend, Tiger. She's a sweet little yellow bird."

34

"Woof! Woof! Nice to meet you, Tiger."

"Chirp. Tweet. My pleasure to meet you."

"Would you like to help with the decorations Nicki?"
Mrs. Jones asks.

"Woof!"

"Here are some flowers and pink and white decorations.
Feel free to use what you want."

"How fun. Woof! Woof! I love your table settings.
How beautiful."

"Thank you."

"Tweet, tweet. I will help you with the flowers."

The Artist Lady pokes her head out and says, "The food and tea are ready." She signals Mrs. Jones to come talk to her.

"We are all ready for our guests, thanks to the both of you. Now, I must get ready. Please excuse me for just a moment and make yourselves comfortable."

Off Mrs. Jones goes to see the Artist Lady.

"Woof! Woof!"

"Tweet! Tweet!"

"Chirp! Chirp!"

Wag! Wag!

MAIL

5712

Ding dong—the doorbell rings.

"Someone is here. I'll get the door," Mrs. Jones says.

"It's Midnight."

"Hello, Midnight. Come in. You look wonderful. How are you?"

"Squeak! Squeak!"

"It's so nice of you to come. Let me introduce you to the others."

"Midnight, you know Tiger, the little yellow bird, and this is Nicki the terrier."

"Squeak! Squeak!"

"I will put you down here so you can visit."

Ding dong—the doorbell rings.

"That must be Jax, the squirrel. I'll go let him in."

42

"Welcome, Jax. I'm so glad you could come. Your tail is so handsome. Please come in and meet everyone."

"Jax, this is Tiger the little yellow bird,

Nicki the terrier,

and Midnight the hamster.

44

Everyone, this is the gray squirrel named Jax. He loves to play hide and surprise when I go on my walks by his tree."

"Woof! Woof!"

"Tweet! Tweet!"

"Squeak! Squeak!"

"Ch, ch, ch, ch, ch!" Jax replies.

"Come, sit down and we shall have some tea," Mrs. Jones says as she shows the guests to the table.

46

They all move to the table and sit down. Mrs. Jones places Midnight next to her. Tiger flies onto her perch.

Mrs. Jones takes out two special little napkins and sets one by each of them. All of the others place their napkins in their laps.

Out comes the Artist Lady without her hat pushing a cart full of nuts, seeds, carrots, cookie bones, and tea with lemon, sugar, and honey on the side.

She places a tray on each end of the table, turns to Mrs. Jones, and says, "Mrs. Jones, you look so lovely today for your tea party with your pretty hat."

"Chirp! Tweet!"

"Woof! Woof!"

"Squeak! Squeak!"

"Ch, ch, ch, ch, ch!"

everyone replies.

Mrs. Jones smiles at the Artist Lady as she pours the tea for her company and offers them the treats.

She places an extra bowl of cookie bones in the center of the table. After all, what would Mrs. Jones tea party be without her cookie bones?

It was a joyous tea party.

They all enjoyed a lovely afternoon sitting in a beautiful place with plenty of food and with new and old friends.

THE END

Once your formal invitations are out, it's time to get ready for tea time.

Tea Time Manners

Remember: The very best host always makes her guests feel good.

Make sure you are ready on time.

Turn off your cell phone.

Introduce your guests to make them feel part of the group.

When everyone is seated, place your napkin in your lap.

Rest your hands in your lap, not on the table.

Avoid burping or making other rude sounds.

When stirring the tea, try not to clink the sides of the cup.

If your tea is hot, never blow on it. Wait until it cools.

Keep your pinky relaxed when drinking tea.

dog gone good tea

CookIe BoNe

Do not slurp your tea.

Dishes should be passed from right to left.

Take no more than three items on your plate. You can always have seconds.

Take small bites. Chew and swallow completely before sipping your tea.

Never talk with food in your mouth.

When you finish eating, leave your utensils on your plate.

Never use a toothpick or dental floss at the table.

Remember to say please and thank you.

The most important function is to socialize with friends, **relax, and enjoy!**

Mrs. Jones is the name of a special dog with lots of special animal friends. She loves to play with them and would love to get her friends together, but they are so different in size and the way they play, some rough, some gentle.

One day, Mrs. Jones thinks of a way to get her friends together—a formal tea party! It would be a pleasant visit with no chasing or rolling in the dirt, but can they all mind their manners?

Mrs. Jones is a Puli, a Hungarian herding dog. She is very pleasant, gentle and has made lots of very different friends.

Tiger the yellow bird is artistic and loves bright colors. Because she can fly off, she doesn't put up with rude behavior.

Nicki the Terrier likes to play and sometimes plays rough. He often grabs food out of a hand or off a plate.

Jax the squirrel is a big tease. He is fast and can run up a tree and chatter a laugh after he plays a trick on someone.

Midnight the hamster is very shy but friendly. He sometimes needs a little encouragement to join in a conversation.

Mrs. Jones is a real dog and Kristi, the author, belongs to her. She is a Puli, a Hungarian herding dog, also used as a guard dog because they are very protective. Female Pulis weigh 20-30 pounds and Mrs. Jones is on the small side. Mrs. Jones is all black. Pulis also come in all white and, rarely, a pale-yellow color called "Champaign". Mrs. Jones had one puppy and it was Champaign. Every animal character in this book has been an actual friend of the real Mrs. Jones. Her website is:
www.mrsjonesadventures.com

Kristi Soli, author, has been aviator, inventor, entrepreneur and artist. She really does have several pretty hats. She got her Bachelor's Degree in Aviation Science at the University of North Dakota and flew airplanes for many years before inventing products. This book is her latest and was inspired by the antics of Mrs. Jones. Kristi's art is abstract oil paintings, which would not have worked for this book. She lives in Minneapolis with Mrs. Jones and they love walking around the nearby lake. Her website is:
www.kristisoli.com

Sharon Wagner, illustrator, grew up on a farm nestled amidst the drift-less hills of Wisconsin, where she found that she loves drawing and painting. She followed her dream, getting a Bachelor of Fine Arts degree at the University of Wisconsin, Stout, and moved to Minneapolis, which has a great art community. Sharon has illustrated several books and produced award winning artwork. She is writing a dark, supernatural thriller, Chorus of the Crows and loves the jungles of Central America. Her website is: **www.sharonwagnerillustration.blogspot.com**

About the Puli: In Hungary, they say "It's not a dog, it's a Puli". They are naturally very protective, affectionate and so smart that they train humans rather than the other way around. They also play tricks on humans and each other and are as playful as puppies their whole lives. As with any pet, owning a Puli is a big commitment.

The dog illustrated in this book does not really look like a Puli because the solid color and fluffy fur would make it impossible to show facial expressions. Live Pulis (called Pulik in Hungary) display expression well, but it does not show in pictures or drawings.

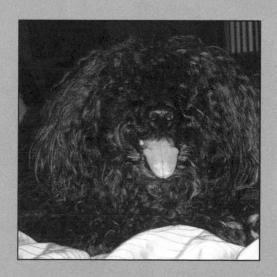